Even Fairies FART

Olives

Words by JENNIFER STINSON   Pictures by REBECCA ASHDOWN

HARPER
An Imprint of HarperCollinsPublishers

Even Fairies Fart

Text copyright © 2017 by Jennifer Stinson

Illustrations copyright © 2017 by Rebecca Ashdown

All rights reserved. Manufactured in China.

www.harpercollinschildrens.com

ISBN 978-0-06-243623-8

The artist used pencil crayons, acrylic inks, and a computer to make the illustrations for this book.

Typography by Rachel Zegar

17 18 19 20 21   SCP   10 9 8 7 6 5 4 3 2 1

❖

First Edition

This book is dedicated to anyone
who ever thought they had to be perfect
—J.S.

For Luce, who taught me how to laugh at myself!
—R.A.

In fairy tales,
things always feel
more perfect than in life.
The dashing prince will find
the fairest maiden for his wife.

The Pixies sprinkle magic dust.

The bluebirds help bake pies.

The pirates find a treasure chest

that sparkles in their eyes.

It all seems so amazing!
Can't we be perfect too?
If we wish on the brightest star,
could all this stuff come true?

Well—

There's more to all these stories.
I promise. Cross my heart.
You might be shocked to hear this,

but even fairies
fart!

POOF!

Yes, fairies fart the same as us,

and goblins stain their clothes.

This dragon cheats
at every game.

Fair maiden
goes here.

That princess picks her nose.

Big bad wolves fall on their snouts.

When pirates lose they brood.

Elves don't always reach the bathroom.
Knights are known to waste their food.

Oops...

OIL

Gnomes will brag that
they're the best,

and trolls are told,
"Time out!"

Unicorns get scared at night,
while wizards mope and pout.

Witches can be very whiny.

Kings and queens don't share.

Monsters sometimes want their mommies.

Mermaids HATE to comb their hair.

When giants go to parties,
they cause a giant scene.
Their table manners are the worst
that you have ever seen!

They gobble cake, they guzzle milk,
and when they start to laugh,
the milk squirts out their noses
and gives everyone a bath!

So if you fart or fuss or fail
or belch or beg or boast,
or think that you're the single kid
who messes up the most,

now you can remind yourself
that simply can't be true.
Everybody everywhere
is quite a lot like

YOU!

In living rooms and castles,
kingdoms near and far away,
fairies fart the same as us.
And who cares?

POOF!

We love them anyway.